Grumpy Badger's Christmas

For Yvonne, who is never grumpy – P B

For Dylan – J C

Original edition published in English by Little Tiger Press, an imprint of
Magi Publications, London, England, 2009.

ISBN 978-0-545-28841-5

Copyright © 2009 by Good Books, Intercourse, PA 17534.
Text copyright © 2009 by Paul Bright.
Illustrations copyright © 2009 by Jane Chapman. All rights reserved.
Published by Scholastic Inc., 557 Broadway, New York, NY 10012, by
arrangement with Little Tiger Press, an imprint of Magi Publications.
SCHOLASTIC and associated logos are trademarks and/or
registered trademarks of Scholastic Inc.

12 11 10 9 8 7 6 5 4 3 2 1   10 11 12 13 14 15/0

Printed in the U.S.A.   08

This edition first printing, September 2010

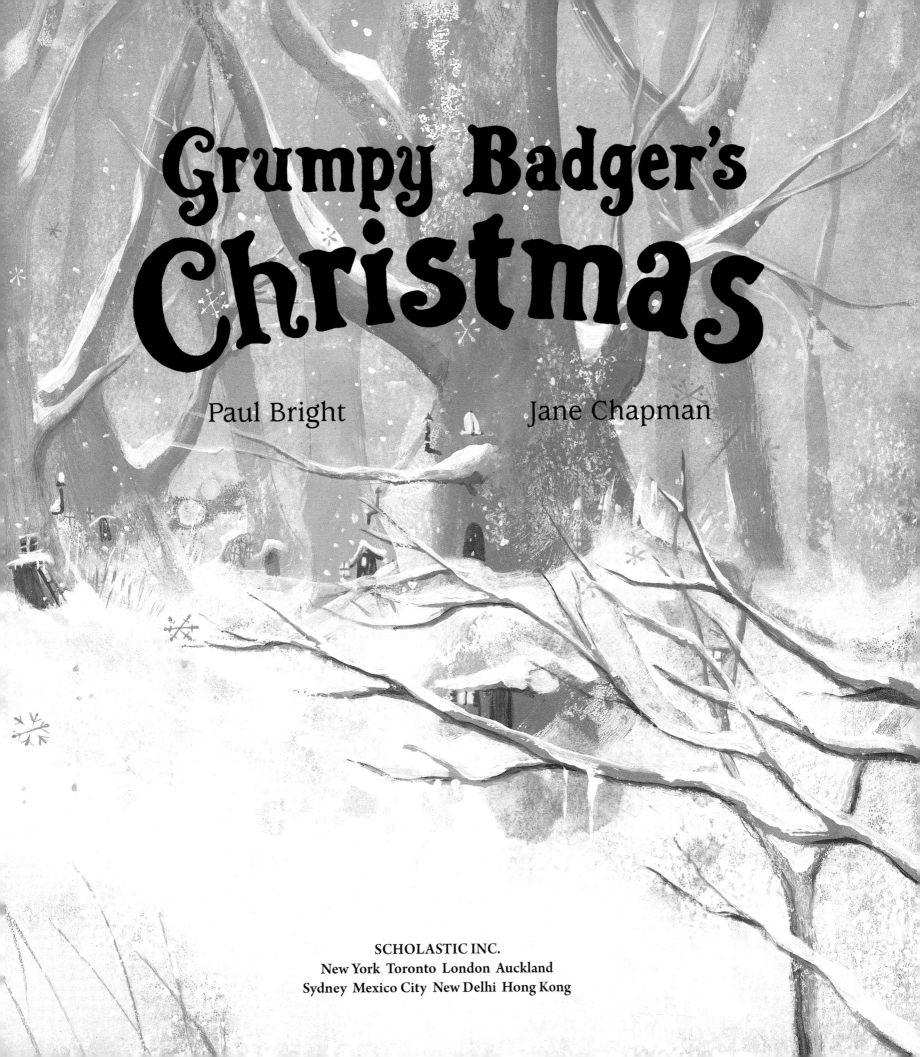

Grumpy Badger's
Christmas

Paul Bright　　　　　Jane Chapman

SCHOLASTIC INC.
New York Toronto London Auckland
Sydney Mexico City New Delhi Hong Kong

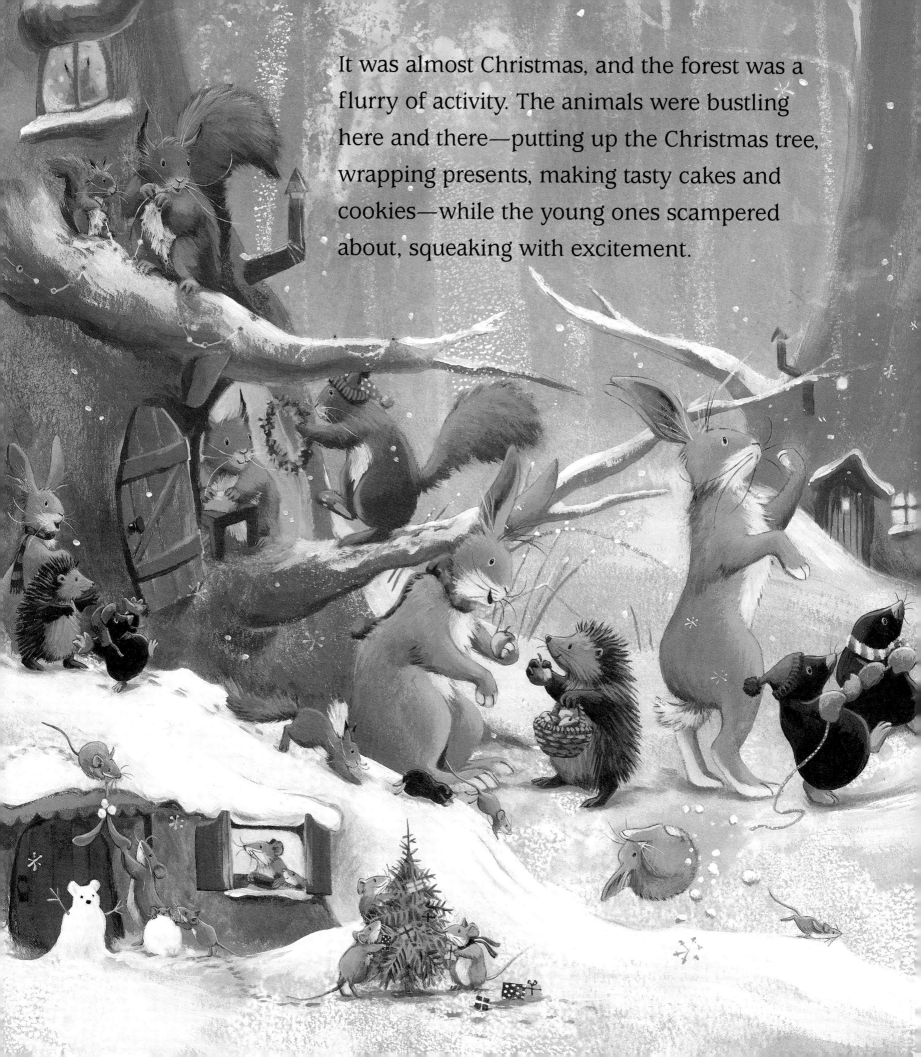

It was almost Christmas, and the forest was a flurry of activity. The animals were bustling here and there—putting up the Christmas tree, wrapping presents, making tasty cakes and cookies—while the young ones scampered about, squeaking with excitement.

Everybody was looking
forward to Christmas.
Well, *almost* everybody . . .

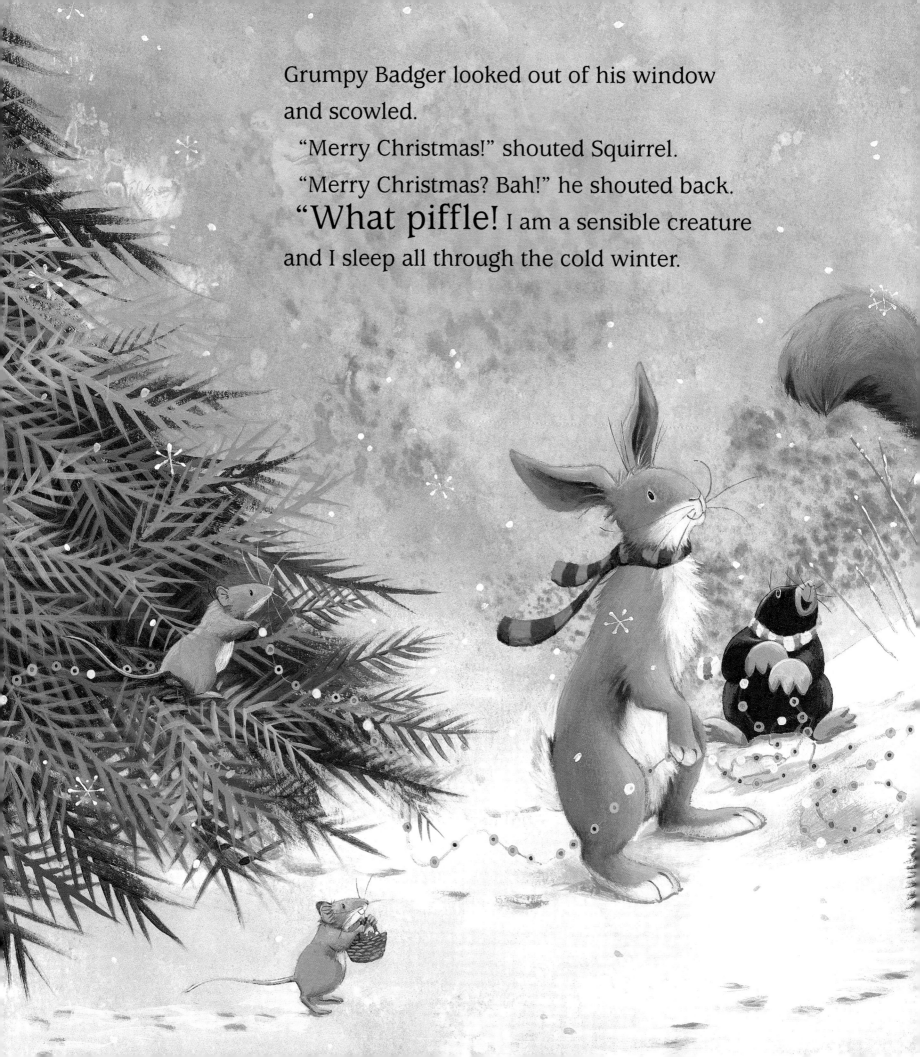

Grumpy Badger looked out of his window
and scowled.

"Merry Christmas!" shouted Squirrel.

"Merry Christmas? Bah!" he shouted back.
"What piffle! I am a sensible creature
and I sleep all through the cold winter.

"Now I am going to bed until the spring, and if anyone wakes me I shall be very, very grumpy!" And with that, he pulled his window shut with a

CLUNK!

Grumpy Badger knew he would be hungry when he woke, so he checked his pantry. There were pies and pastries, hams and cheeses, crispy crackers, jars of fruit and sticky-sweet jams.

"That *should* do," he said.

Then he filled his hot water bottle
and climbed into bed.

He had just closed his eyes when
there was a knock at the door.

KNOCK!
KNOCK!
KNOCK!

It was Mole.

"M-m-merry Christmas, Mr. Badger," he said,
timidly. "I'm sorry to bother you. I've been trying
to put lights on the Christmas tree, but it's just
too big. Could I please borrow your ladder?"

"Christmas tree?" spluttered Grumpy Badger. "Piffle and double piffle! Christmas is for sleeping—and that's what I'm trying to do!" And he closed the door with a

BANG!

"Bah!" huffed Grumpy Badger, climbing into bed. "Borrow my ladder indeed! All I want is a bit of peace and quiet, so leave me alone!"

He peeked under his bed, where he'd put more food for springtime: candies and cornbread and cherry cupcakes.

Then he cuddled deep into his big, warm comforter. He was just starting to snore when there was another knock at the door.

KNOCK!

KNOCK!

KNOCK!

This time it was Squirrel.
"Hello, Badger," he said,
cheerily. "I've brought you
a Christmas present."

"Christmas present?" snorted Grumpy Badger.

"Piffle and triple piffle!

I don't like presents and I don't like Christmas!
All I want is a little peace!" And he shut the
door with a **CRASH!**

Now Grumpy Badger was really grumpy. To cheer himself up, he thought about the bottles and bottles of homemade lemonade he had in the cellar. Then he lay down and closed his eyes. But he couldn't sleep—his head felt a little chilly.

Suddenly there was a loud banging at the door.

BANG!
BANG!
BANG!

"Oh, what is it *now*?" Grumpy Badger sighed. He was about as tired and grumpy as a Badger can be.

"Oh, Badger," panted Rabbit. "Help! It's poor Mole. He's stuck at the top of the Christmas tree. Come quickly!"

"PIFFLE!" shouted Grumpy Badger. "And triple piffle on top of that! Why can't everyone just leave me alone?" And he slammed the door so hard that the whole house shook!

SLAM!

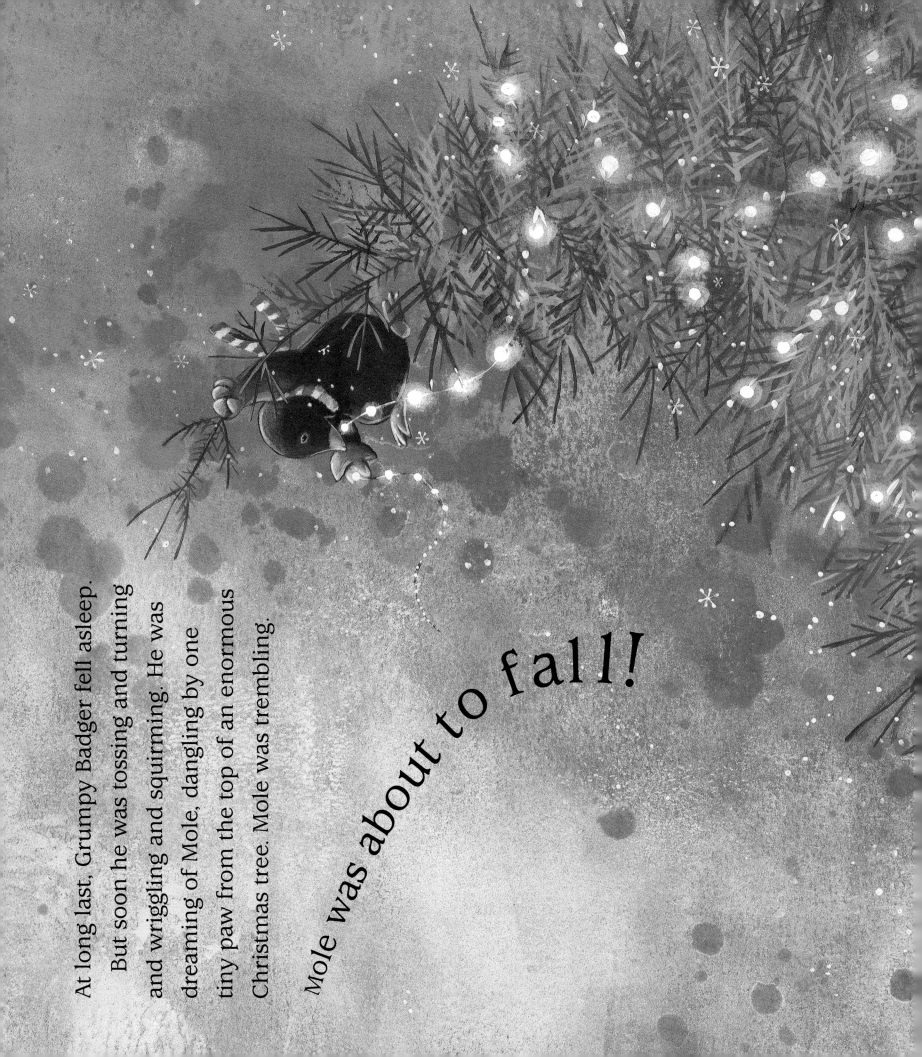

At long last, Grumpy Badger fell asleep.
But soon he was tossing and turning
and wriggling and squirming. He was
dreaming of Mole, dangling by one
tiny paw from the top of an enormous
Christmas tree. Mole was trembling.

Mole was about to fall!

"NOOOOOO!"
screamed Grumpy Badger,
sitting bolt upright, and
suddenly wide awake.

"What have I done?"

He jumped out of bed, grabbed his ladder
and dashed into the street.

Grumpy Badger raced up to
the Christmas tree.
    "Hold on, Mole!" he cried.

He scrambled up the
ladder, scooped Mole
gently into his arms,
then helped him
down to the ground.

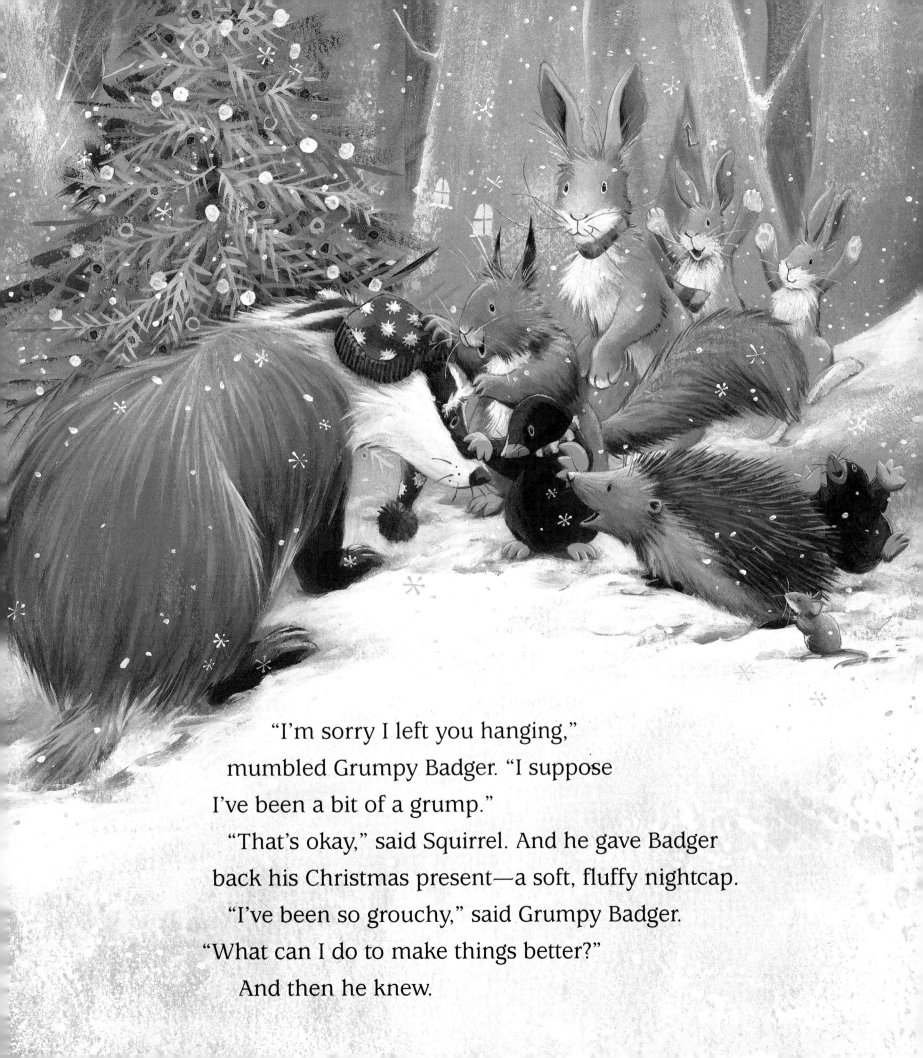

"I'm sorry I left you hanging,"
mumbled Grumpy Badger. "I suppose
I've been a bit of a grump."

"That's okay," said Squirrel. And he gave Badger
back his Christmas present—a soft, fluffy nightcap.

"I've been so grouchy," said Grumpy Badger.
"What can I do to make things better?"

And then he knew.

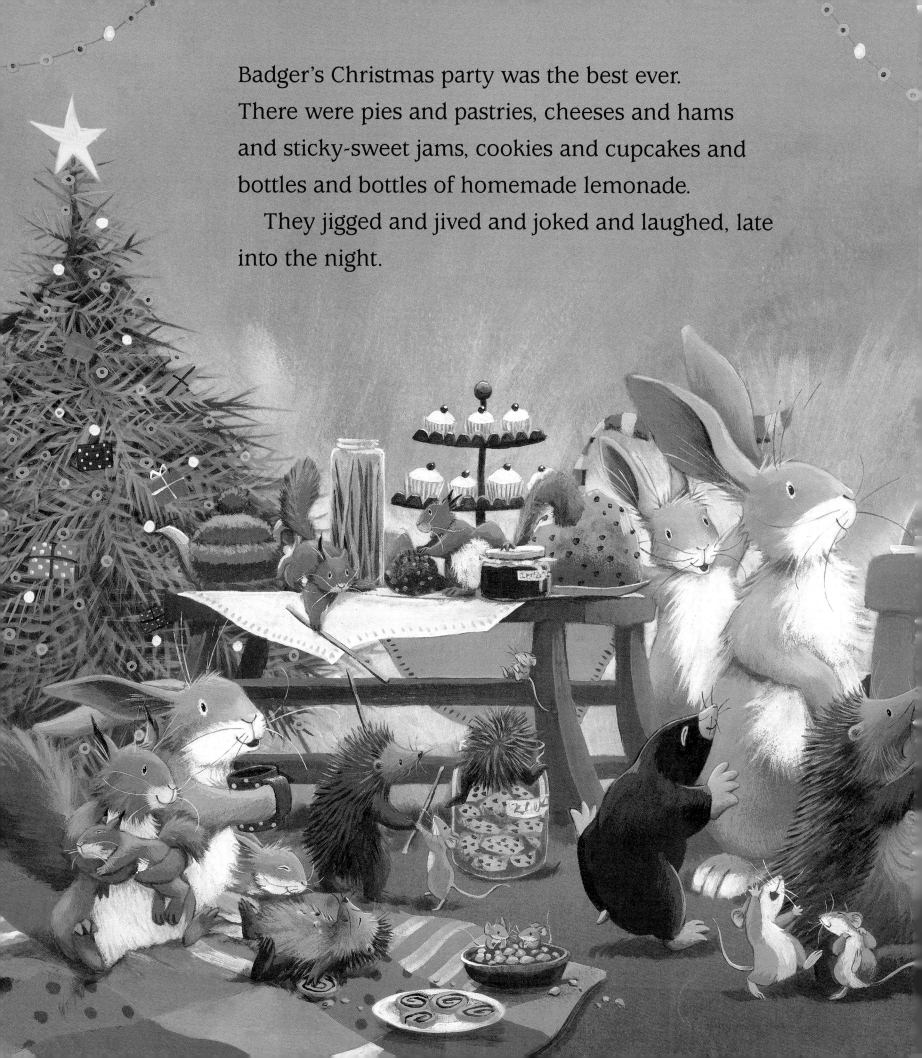

Badger's Christmas party was the best ever. There were pies and pastries, cheeses and hams and sticky-sweet jams, cookies and cupcakes and bottles and bottles of homemade lemonade.

They jigged and jived and joked and laughed, late into the night.

"Merry Christmas, everybody!" Badger cried. "And if you don't all come to my party next year,

I SHALL BE
VERY
GRUMPY
INDEED!"